HAPPY BIRTHDAY

DON'T ASK A DINOSAUR

BY DEBORAH BRUSS & MATT FORREST ESENWINE
ILLUSTRATED BY LOUIE CHIN

POW!

Brooklyn, NY

If you're going to plan
a birthday party,
stop and think it through.
Be careful
what you dare
to ask
to do.

Don't ask **a Ty·ra·nno·sau·rus Rex** to try to wrap a gift,

or
ask
a Saur·o·po·sei·don
for just
a "little" lift.

Don't ask
an An·ky·lo·sau·rus
to come in through the gate,

or ask **a Tan·y·stro·phe·us** to help you decorate.

Tri·ce·ra·tops will not be pleased with just one party hat.

Chances are,
Sty·ra·co·sau·rus
will want *more* than that!

Don't ask a **Li·o·pleur·o·don** to bake your birthday cake, or ask a **Car·no·taur** to frost it...

...what
a mess
he'd make!

The·re·zi·no·sau·rus
shouldn't blow up
the balloons.

Don't ask
an Ar·gen·ti·no·sau·rus
to play
hide-and-seek.

I·gua·na·don
should not be asked
to paint your
nose or cheek.

Don't dare ask a
Dip·lo·do·cus
if he would care
to dance.

You could ask **Pach·y·ceph·a·lo·saur** — but no, don't take a chance!

So when you plan a birthday party, stop and think it through.

and then
they'll all
join in...

to help you
blow your
candles...

...out.

Glossary

Ankylosaurus
"Fused lizard"
Ank-EYE-low-SAWR-us

One of the widest dinosaurs, Ankylosaurus was built like an armoured tank.

Argentinosaurus
"Argentina lizard"
AR-jen-TEE-no-SAWRE-us

Argentinosaurus was probably the heaviest dinosaur of all. It weighed more than 1,500 people.

Carnotaurus
"Meat eating bull"
CAR-no-TORE-us

Also known as a Carnotaur, this carnivorous (meat-eating) dinosaur had very tiny arms—even smaller than T. Rex's—so frosting a cake might be hard to do.

Deinocheirus
"Terrible hand"
DIE-noh-KIRE-us

One of the strangest looking dinosaurs, Deinocheirus had very large hands, big feet, and probably a row of spines, or sail, running down the length of his back.

Diplodocus
"Double beam"
Dip-LOW-doe-cus

Diplodocus was probably the longest dinosaur, and had a whip-like tail with 80 vertebrae. Compared to the rest of its body, its head was very small—about the size of a horse's head.

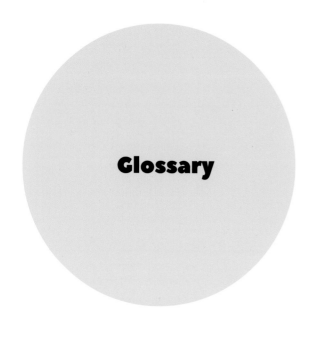

Iguanodon
"Iguana tooth"
Ig-WAH-no-don

Iguanodon had funny looking hands with a thumb like a large spike, not useful for holding a paint brush.

Liopleurodon
"Smooth-sided teeth"
LEE-oh-PLUR-oh-don

With four large, paddle-like feet and a huge head filled with sharp teeth, Liopleurodon would have been better at eating cake, than baking it.

Pachycephalosaur
"Thick-headed lizard"
PACK-ee-SEF-ah-low-sawr

Pachycephalosaur, the bone-head of dinosaurs, had a skull that was nearly a foot thick in the front. Watch out if he starts headbanging on the dance floor!

Sauroposeidon
"Earthquake god lizard"
SAWR-uh-poe-SIE-don

Sauroposeidon was probably the tallest dinosaur. With a 56-foot-long neck, it was taller than nine men standing on each other's shoulders.

Styracosaurus
"Spiked lizard"
sty-RACK-oh-SAWR-us

With spiky horns all over Styracosaurus' head, birthday balloons wouldn't stand a chance.

Tanystropheus
"Long strap"
tan-ee-STROH-fee-us

With a neck that was half of its entire body's length, scientists believe Tanystropheus was very good at snatching fish from the water.

Therezinosaurus
"Reaping Lizard"
ther-uh-ZEEN-oh-SAWR-us

With a duck-bill skull, large arms, and extremely long claws (up to 3 feet!), Therezinosaurus was one of the oddest-looking dinosaurs. And although it might have been scary-looking, scientists believe it was a plant-eater.

Triceratops
"Three-horned face"
tri-SER-uh-tops

A relative of Anchiceratops and Styracosaurus, Triceratops had a massive head, about four times bigger than the head of Diplodocus, the longest dinosaur.

Tyrannosaurus Rex
"Tyrant lizard king"
Tie-RAN-o-SAWR-us rex

Not only did the T. Rex have short arms, it only had two fingers on each hand...not very useful for wrapping presents!

Don't Ask a Dinosaur

Text © 2018 by Matt Forrest Esenwine & Deborah Bruss
Illustrations © 2018 by Louie Chin

Published by POW!
a division of powerHouse Packaging & Supply, Inc.
32 Adams Street, Brooklyn, NY 11201-1021
info@powkidsbooks.com · www.powkidsbooks.com
www.powerHouseBooks.com · www.powerHousePackaging.com

Printed and bound by Tien Wah Press

Library of Congress Control Number: 2017963831

ISBN: 978-1-57687-841-5

10 9 8 7 6 5 4 3 2 1

Printed in Malaysia

For Greyson, whose love of dinosaurs is exceeded only by the gentleness of his heart.
—M. F. E.

For Nathanial and Isaac, who showed me that no matter what happens, birthday parties can be a blast.
— D. B.

For my mom,
禤翠芳
and my grandma,
張艷其
— L.C.